This Bob the Builder Annual belongs to

....

Bob the Builder™

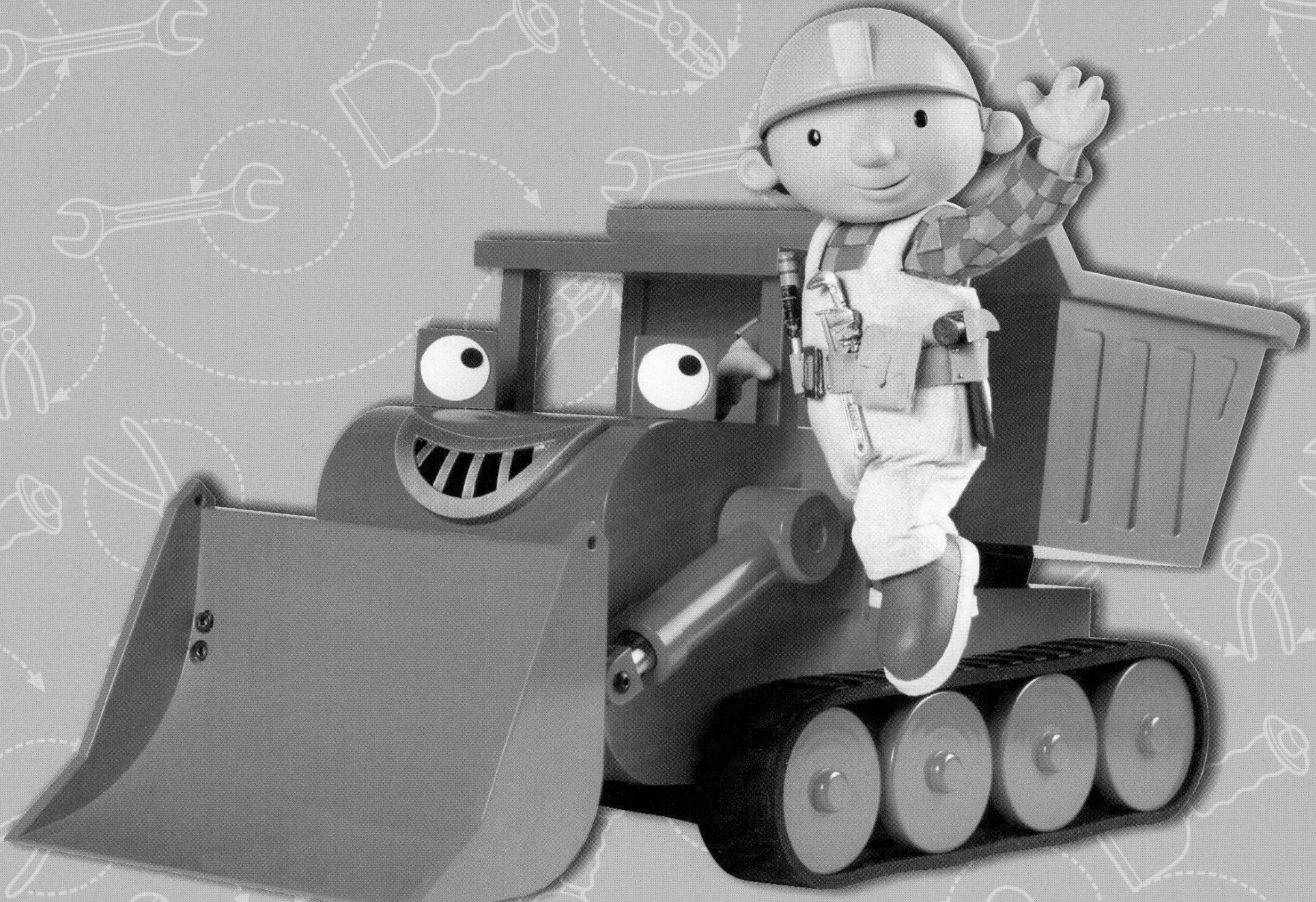

First published in Great Britain in 2009
by Egmont UK Ltd, 239 Kensington High Street, London W8 6SA

EGMONT
We bring stories to life

Based on the television series Bob the Builder © 2009 HIT Entertainment Limited
and Keith Chapman. All rights reserved. The Bob the Builder name and character,
related characters and the Bob figure and riveted logo are trademarks of
HIT Entertainment Limited.
Reg. U.S. Pat. & ™. Off. and in the UK and other countries.

Written by Penny Worms. Designed by Graham Rich.

ISBN 978 1 4052 4637 8
1 3 5 7 9 10 8 6 4 2
Printed in Italy

Contents

A Year in Sunflower Valley

Bob the Builder here. Welcome to Sunflower Valley. The team and I have been busy all year. I have a brand new house. My machines have a super-dry shelter. And Bobland Bay now has shops, a new promenade and an ice-cream parlour!

Here's how it happened . . .

Meet the Machine Team

Bob has a trusted team of machines that helps him with all his building projects. Each machine has special skills.

Lofty

Lofty is a mobile crane. He has three favourite tools: a grabber, an electro-magnet and a demolition ball.

- MULTI-SKILLED ✓
- DEMOLITION ✓
- STRENGTH ✓
- LIFTING ✓
- CARRYING ✓

Scoop

Scoop is the team leader. He is a digger, who can also move and lift heavy things.

- LEADERSHIP ✓
- DIGGING ✓
- STRENGTH ✓
- LIFTING ✓
- CARRYING ✓

Scrambler

Scrambler is an all-terrain quad bike. He takes Bob wherever he needs to go – fast!

- SPEEDY ✓
- OFF-ROAD ✓
- MANOEUVRABLE ✓

Dizzy

Dizzy is a cement mixer. She mixes all the ingredients in her drum and pours cement where it's needed.

- MIXING ✓
- LEADERSHIP ✓
- RELIABILITY ✓
- GOOD IDEAS ✓

Roley

Roley is a steamroller. He can flatten uneven ground and smooth surfaces such as new roads.

ROLLING ✓
FLATTENING ✓
STRENGTH ✓

Muck

Muck is a digger-dumper. His tracks mean he can go over uneven ground and he does lots of heavy work.

STRENGTH ✓
DIGGING ✓
CARRYING ✓
OFF-ROAD ✓

Benny

Benny is a robo-digger. He's small, nippy and good at doing lots of different jobs – all at the same time!

MULTI-SKILLED ✓
DIGGING ✓
LIFTING ✓
OFF-ROAD ✓
MANOEUVRABLE ✓

Tumbler

Tumbler is a large motorised cement mixer. He helps when Bob and the team need lots of cement!

MIXING ✓
CARRYING ✓
STRENGTH ✓

Packer

Packer is an articulated lorry. He has different trailers and can carry big loads!

CARRYING ✓
REFRIGERATION ✓
STRENGTH ✓

Sumsy

Sumsy is Farmer Pickles' fork-lift truck. He pulls a useful trailer whenever it is needed.

LIFTING ✓
CARRYING ✓
MANOEUVRABLE ✓

Guess Who

Who is this?

a) Wendy

b) Flora

c) Mrs Bentley

Who is this?

a) Sandy Creek

b) Farmer Pickles

c) Mayor Bentley

Who is this?

a) Marjorie at the sunflower factory

b) Ela the teacher

c) Meg at the dairy

Who is this?

a) Lewella, the hotel owner

b) Mrs Sabatini

c) Ela the teacher

All these people live and work in Bobsville or Bobland Bay. Do you know their names?

Who is this?

a) Scruffty

b) Pilchard

c) Spud

Who is this?

a) Mayor Bentley

b) Mr Beasley

c) Farmer Pickles

Who is this?

a) Chip Chipper

b) Dickie Chester, hotel manager

c) Sandy Creek

Who is this?

a) Mr Sabatini

b) Paolo, Mr Sabatini's brother

c) The hotel chef

Answers on page 68.

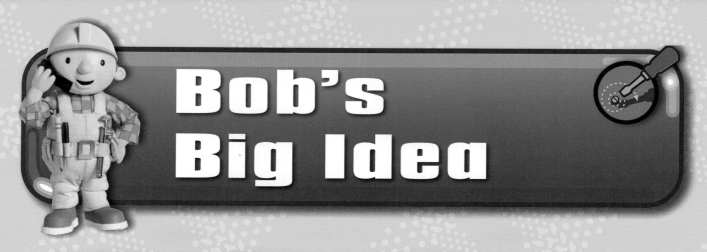

Bob's Big Idea

It was early morning in Sunflower Valley. Wendy and the team were excited. They had decided to build Bob his very own house. Bob had been sleeping in Scoop's digger for a week. He needed a more comfortable place to sleep. "What sort of house are we going to build, Bob?" asked Scoop.

Bob couldn't decide. He had built so many houses, he wasn't sure what he'd like for himself.

"I know!" said Wendy. "What about a house that looks like no other house in the Valley. A Bob house!"

The machines loved that idea. Wendy gave Bob a catalogue. Bob just had to say what pieces he wanted to use. There was so much choice!

"We could start the foundations," suggested Lofty, "while Bob chooses."

The team worked together to lay the foundations.

Bob had to choose the walls. He couldn't make up his mind. Dizzy suggested big windows to let in lots of light, while Lofty and Roley suggested a big balcony with steps going up to it.

Bob thought these were brilliant ideas.

Wendy wrote down what they needed.

"Come on, you lot!" she said. "Let's go and get all the bits."

They drove off, leaving Bob to think about what else he'd like for his dream home.

When they returned, they put all the pieces on the ground.

"Gosh!" said Bob. "It's going to be a big house, isn't it?"

"Yes," said Scoop. **"Can we build it?"**

"Yes, we can!" the team cried.

They set to work. Bob and Wendy laid the floor. Scoop and Muck built the walls. Then Lofty lowered the upstairs floor into place. The house locked together easily when everyone worked together.

The house was almost finished.

"It looks great, team!" said Bob with delight. "You've all had some brilliant ideas. I just wish one of them was mine!"

"Never mind," laughed Scoop. "You can choose the roof."

Bob thought for a long time.

"I know!" said Muck, wanting to help. "If the roof is really wide, the bits that hang over will give shade!"

"Ooh, yes!" said Wendy, joining in. "And if the gutters stick out, the rainwater will fall down …"

"Into a pond!" cried Roley. Better still, Bob could have a stream running all the way round the house. He could have fish!

The end result looked incredible! They were such great ideas.

Bob was more determined than ever to come up with something for his new house. He took Scrambler to look at all the houses he had built around Sunflower Valley. He might get inspiration from one of them. He just wished he could see all the houses in one go.

Then Bob had an idea! He could build a glass tower on the house. Then he could look over the whole Valley and admire what they had built together.

"Oh, my," said Wendy when it was finished. "This was the best idea yet, Bob!" The view of the Valley was wonderful.

"It's not who has the ideas," said Bob. "It's being a team that's important."

Wendy agreed. They knew they couldn't have done any of this without their friends. They were part of the best building team ever!

Who Lives Where?

Help Bob, Spud and Lofty find their way home, without going through a no-entry sign.

Answers on page 68.

Colour In Scrambler

Bob and Scrambler are whizzing round Sunflower Valley together.
Can you colour them in?

Roley Takes the Blame

It had been raining for days in Sunflower Valley. There were puddles everywhere and the ground was very muddy.

"I'm glad we've got a nice dry shelter," said Lofty.

But Muck was delighted it had been raining. "Neeeow!" he cried as he sped into the homestead. "Mucky Muck! King of the Skidsies!" he called as he slid on the mud. He turned sharply and came to a halt in front of the shelter.

"I bet I could skid even further!" said Roley.

"No way!" said Muck, doing an even longer skid.

The others were worried. They said it was dangerous.

Muck teased Roley, asking him if that's why he didn't try it.

"Just watch me!" said Roley.

He backed up so he could pick up enough speed to do a really good skid. Then he went full throttle towards the mud.

"Skidsieeeees!" he yelled as he slammed on his brakes. He tried to turn, but lost control …

Roley smashed into the main upright of the shelter, bringing the whole thing tumbling down.

The loud CRASH! woke up Bob.

"What on earth was that?" he said, appearing in his pyjamas. Wendy came out of her caravan. They both looked at the destroyed shelter.

Dizzy was very cross with Roley. "I knew skidsies were dangerous!"

"I'm sorry, Bob," said Roley, very upset.

"You need to be careful," said Bob trying to calm everyone down. "We'll just have to build a new shelter. And make it skidsie proof!" He went back inside to get dressed.

Roley turned on Muck. "Why didn't you tell Bob it was your fault?" he grumbled.

"My fault?" said Muck, taken aback.

"Yeah," said Roley. "You made me do a skidsie."

Before Muck could reply, Bob reappeared with a plan for a new shelter. Each machine had their own place and some had special roller shutter doors.

"Can we build it?"

"Yes, we can!"

Scoop helped with the foundations. Bob and Wendy bolted together the beams. The others lifted the metal sheeting into place.

"But there aren't enough places for everyone," said Dizzy, looking at what they had built so far.

Bob explained that Dizzy and Scrambler were going to have places upstairs and get to them by a machine ramp!

"That's Muck-tastic!" cried Muck.

"Well, you won't be going up it," Roley said grumpily.

Dizzy had had enough of their squabbling. "Why don't you do something useful, like move the garage doors?" she suggested.

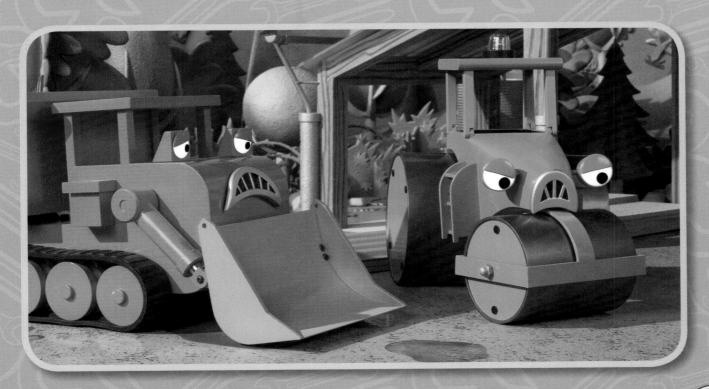

"Hey! They're our colours!" cried Muck, picking up the red door. Roley bumped into him, desperate to see if there was a green one. Muck dropped his door on to some beams.

"That's what our ramp is going to be like!" said Dizzy excitedly.

Roley teased Muck, saying "Perhaps you'd like to try this one?"

"But the door isn't a proper ramp …" said Muck.

"Oh, right," said Roley. "You make me knock down a whole shelter, but you're too afraid to go up a silly little ramp."

Muck decided to show Roley he wasn't afraid. "Mucky Muck is going up," said Muck, speeding up the ramp, but the door buckled under his weight.

"Look what your silly arguing has done now!" said Dizzy.

Both Roley and Muck felt terrible. Roley told Bob it was all his fault, but Muck said it was *his* fault. Bob, Wendy and Dizzy couldn't believe they were now arguing about who was to blame!

"I'm going to let you have my space!" Roley said to Muck, generously. He didn't want Muck getting wet because of him.

But when the garages were finally finished, Bob and Wendy closed *all* the doors, including a shiny red one!

"I had a spare door," Bob explained. "All I needed to do was paint it red. Now no one will get wet!"

Roley and Muck were so pleased to be friends again, and they vowed never to do skidsies in front of this shelter, ever!

Here are Bob, Wendy and Lofty all working together to build Bob a dream home.

There are five differences between this picture and the one opposite. Can you spot them?

Answers on page 68.

Muck's Machine Wash

One morning, Scrambler and Muck were both playing in the mud.

"They don't call you Mucky Muck for nothing," said Scrambler, skidding and sliding with Muck. "You're the best!"

Wendy didn't share their excitement when she saw how mud-splattered they were. "Bob only cleaned you this morning!" she said. "But don't worry. Soon you'll be able to wash yourselves!"

Muck wondered what she meant but didn't have time to ask. Bob needed him in the yard.

When he got there, Bob was unloading rollers and sponges from Packer's trailer.

"Wow! What's that?" Dizzy asked Bob.

"It's a machine wash," Bob replied. "Wendy and Lofty are going to build it while we dig the foundations for the new houses in Bobland Bay."

All the machines thought the idea of a bubble wash sounded brilliant – all except Muck!

Scrambler wanted Muck to go scrambling again.

"You'll have plenty of time for a scram when we've finished the foundations," Bob said.

"Can we dig them?"

"Yes, we can!"

And leaving Wendy, Lofty and Scrambler, Bob and the others trundled off to Bobland Bay.

Wendy and Lofty began to build the machine wash. When the main frame was up, Wendy laid the floor while Lofty went to get the large rollers.

"Will these rollers be scratchy?" he asked, lowering them into place with his crane attachment.

"No, Lofty," Wendy replied. "I think they will tickle!"

Lofty began to giggle. He was very ticklish!

"Right, Lofty," said Wendy, after the rollers were fixed into place. "Next we need to fit the solar panels. This machine is going to need a lot of energy." The solar panels would collect energy from the sun. And rain would be collected in a barrel and used to wash the machines.

Over in Bobland Bay, Scoop was digging out the foundations for the new Bob houses, while Roley was flattening the rest of the area. Muck was getting mucky!

Bob's mobile rang.

"Hello, Bob the Builder," he said into the phone.

"Hello, Bob, it's Mayor Bentley," said the voice on the other end. "What do you think of 'Come and play in Bobland Bay' for a catchy phrase?"

Bob didn't think it was catchy enough.

"Oh I know, Bob," said the mayor. "I'll pop by later for a bit of inspiration."

"That's a great idea," said Bob.

Once Dizzy had poured all the concrete into the foundations, there was nothing more they could do until it had set.

"Ready for home, everyone?" asked Bob. "Come on, Wendy will be waiting. It's definitely time you had a go in the machine wash, Muck."

Back at the yard, Scrambler was keen to go first. He couldn't stop laughing as the jets of water tickled his chassis.

Muck watched but didn't move.

"We all need a wash at the end of the day, Muck," said Bob kindly. "Besides, you might even like it!"

With everyone looking at him, Muck reluctantly agreed.

"Goodbye, Mucky Muck!" he said, disappearing into the bubbles.

There was a lot of moaning and groaning. Everyone watched anxiously as Muck moved into the blow-dry section.

"I do hope he's OK," said Wendy.

Then suddenly Muck burst out. "Why didn't anyone tell me that getting clean was so much fun!"

Mr Bentley arrived to see all the machines laughing and looking sparkling clean.

"What about this for a catchy phrase …" said the mayor. "'Bobland Bay. Takes your breath away!'"

Wendy and Bob looked unsure.

"What about, 'Fun all day at Bobland Bay!'" suggested Muck. "That's what we've had!"

It summed up Bobland Bay perfectly!

Mucky Muck's Maze

Help Mucky Muck get to the hill to play without having to go through Wendy's machine wash.

Answer on page 68.

The Shapes Game

Spud is playing a game to see how many shapes he can see in Scarecrow Cottage. Can you help him? Write the number of each shape you find in the shape spaces below. Then colour in the picture!

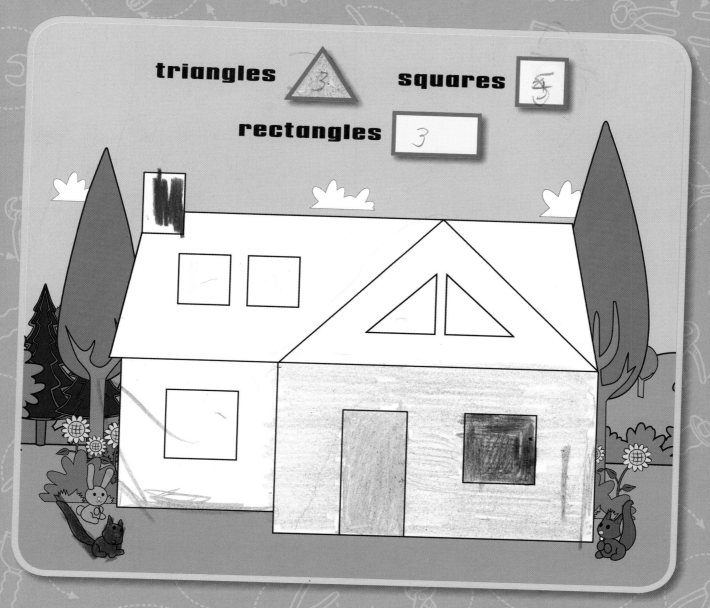

triangles 3   squares 5

rectangles 3

Answers on page 68.

Colour Mix-Up

There has been a colour mix-up in Sunflower Valley. Can you circle the machines that are the correct colour?

Scoop

Muck

Dizzy

Roley

Lofty

Benny

Scrambler

Answers on page 68.

Packer's Trailer Trouble

"It's working!" cried Meg one morning, after Bob had assembled her new ice-cream machine. They both knew this was an important step for Bobland Bay. No seaside town should be without an ice-cream shop!

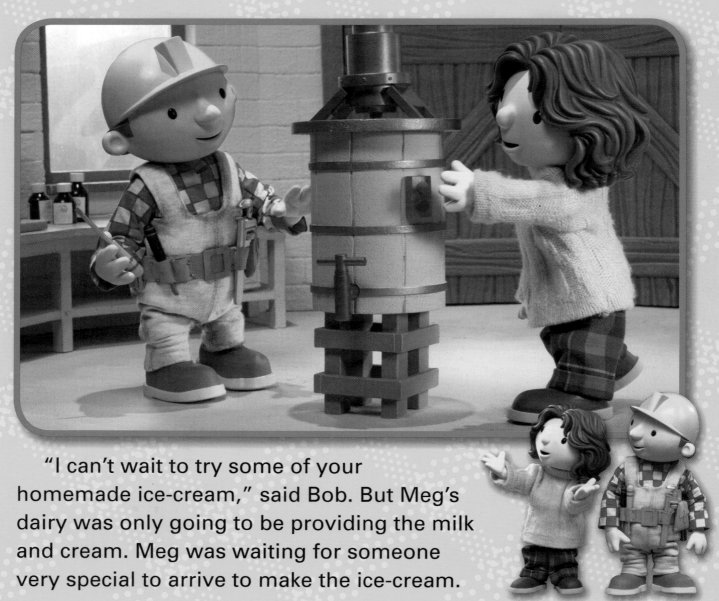

"I can't wait to try some of your homemade ice-cream," said Bob. But Meg's dairy was only going to be providing the milk and cream. Meg was waiting for someone very special to arrive to make the ice-cream.

Outside the dairy, Packer tooted his horn. Meg and Bob rushed out to see Mr Sabatini, the pizza maker, climbing down from Packer's cab. Another man got out from the other side.

"This is my brother, Paolo," said Mr Sabatini, introducing Bob and Meg. "He has-a come to run the new ice-a-cream-a parlour."

"Paolo is famous for making delicious ice-cream," Meg told Bob.

Paolo was delighted to meet Bob.

"Are you building the new ice-a-cream parlour here?" Paolo asked.

"No, we're building it down at Bobland Bay and I'd better head back to help the team."

Packer offered to give Bob a lift. They found Wendy showing the team the plans for the ice-cream parlour.

The machines were curious about the giant ice-cream on top of the planned building.

"Is it real, Bob?" asked Lofty.

"No Lofty," laughed Bob. "Chip Chipper the woodsman is making it for me out of wood."

Packer volunteered to go and collect it. "Packer delivers!" he called as he drove away.

"Right, team," said Bob. **"Can we build it?"**

"Yes, we can!" all the machines replied.

Packer didn't get very far before he met Dodger and Scrambler playing 'Follow-the-leader'. Packer wanted to play!

"This is the best game ever!" said Packer, after following Scrambler through the trees. He had forgotten about Bob's job.

Luckily, Packer was wearing his talkie-talkie.

"Bob to Packer, over," said Bob into the talkie-talkie radio.

Packer suddenly stopped his game. Hearing Bob's voice made him remember the giant ice-cream.

"I'm really sorry, Bob," Packer said. "I'll get it now."

He was about to zoom off when he got a call from Meg. Paolo had made the ice-cream and they needed Packer to pick it up in his refrigerated trailer. Packer decided to do that job first because the dairy was nearer.

When Packer arrived back at the ice-cream parlour, Bob was delighted to see him. "I can't wait to show Meg and Paolo the wooden ice-cream."

"I haven't collected that yet," Packer said. "I've got the real ice-cream!"

Bob and Paolo looked in the back of Packer's trailer.

"Mamma mia!" cried Paolo, looking at all the melted ice-cream.

"You were supposed to pick it up in your refrigerated trailer, remember?" said Wendy.

Packer felt terrible. He had messed everything up.

"You need to remember to finish your jobs before you start playing," said Bob. "But we've still got time. Meg, Paolo, can you make some more ice-cream?"

"We can try," Paolo replied.

Packer took them back to the dairy.

They had lots of milk but not a lot of fruit left. Paolo knew what to do – mix it all together to make Tutti Frutti! They went inside to get started.

Scrambler and Dodger screeched round the corner. They had been following Packer all this time!

"You're a wicked leader," said Dodger. "Shall we play another game?"

"Oh no!" said Packer. He'd learned his lesson. He wasn't going to let Bob down again. "I've got to get my work done first."

"Can we help?" asked Dodger.

Packer suddenly realised how he could make it up to everyone. "Yes, you can!" he said, happily. "Do you know where Chip Chipper lives …?"

The opening of the ice-cream parlour went ahead on time. Dodger and Scrambler had collected the giant ice-cream cone and Lofty lifted it into place. Meg and Paolo had made more delicious ice-cream and Packer had delivered it in his refrigerated trailer.

"I declare this Ice-cream Parlour open," said Mr Bentley.

"Hurray!" everyone cried and they all tucked into their first Bobland Bay ice-cream.

Colour In the Scene

Bob and his team are building a shelter. Can you draw in what you think Lofty is lifting up and then colour in the picture?

The Best Team Ever

You can help to read this story. Listen to the words and when you get to a picture say the name.

Bob   Benny   Scoop   Packer   Sumsy

 needed to build a row of shops in Bobland

Bay. He asked to be in charge of the

'fetching' team and to lead the 'building'

team. said wouldn't know what

to do, but said he'd help .

 had and  in his team.

They went to get the materials. and his

team started with the foundations. When

returned, he couldn't believe that 's team

had finished, and they were calling him

Big Boss !

 was determined to beat next

time. He told and  that they were

going to take a short cut with the next load.

When they were all packed up, and

 were worried. "Are you sure we should

carry all this at once, Team Leader  ?"

"This way we'll finish our job first! " He led

the way through the trees.

"It's really muddy!" said , stopping

at the edge of a field, but ploughed on.

 and watched as 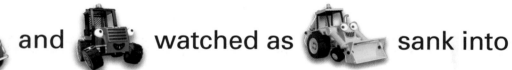 sank into

the mud. He was stuck! called on

his talkie-talkie. was there with in

no time.

"Keep still, ," he called. "We'll soon

have you out of there!" hooked a chain

to  and they pulled out.

"I'm sorry, ," said . "I wanted to

be the best team leader."

 thought of a way to make it up

to . The two teams could get the bits

for the Bobshops together.

"Unreal, banana peel," said to .

They got the job done in record time.

 and 's best team ever!

Whose Wheels?

Whose wheels and tracks are these? Can you match them up to the right machine and then colour in the pictures?

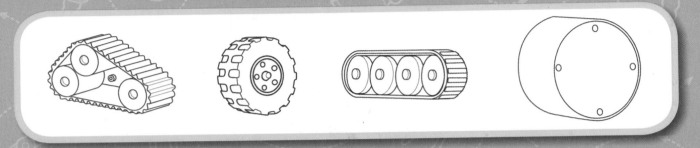

Answer on page 68.

Join the Dots

What is Bob looking for in his tool box? Join the dots, starting at the number '1', to find out. Then you can colour in the picture.

Answer on page 68.

Spud and the Hotel

Spud and Scrambler were off to Bobland Bay to see the new hotel. The main hotel was already built but Bob and his team were building the guest villas next door.

Spud thought he knew all about hotels. "I've worked in a hotel kitchen before."

As Spud and Scrambler arrived, Bob was unveiling the plans.

"This is what it will look like," said Bob.

"Wow!" said Spud. "Does this mean there'll be lots of new visitors to Bobland Bay?"

"Yes, Spud," said Wendy, "and a lovely hotel like this will keep them coming!"

Bob introduced the team to Lewella, the hotel's owner.

"I'm so sorry I can't stay to chat, but the new hotel manager is late and the rooms still haven't got beds." She went off with Packer to Bobsville to pick up everything she needed.

"Right, team," said Bob. "Let's get cracking."

Scoop led the team.

"Can we build it?"
"Yes, we can!"

As everyone set to work, Spud and Scrambler went to have a sneaky peek inside the hotel.

When they got to the front door, a family arrived.

"Hello!" said Spud. "Are you new to Bobland Bay?"

"Yes," answered the little boy, excitedly. "We've come here on our holidays!"

The boy's mother asked Spud if he was the hotel manager. Spud liked the sound of that!

"Yes," he replied. "That's me! Spud the Hotel Manager!"

Scrambler nudged Spud. What was he doing?

Spud picked up the family's bags, saying he would show them to their room.

"I do hope you like it," he said. He struggled up the stairs, but as he stumbled into the room, the bags clattered to the floor.

"At least you don't have to unpack!" he said, brightly.

But then the family noticed there were no beds …

"I'm sorry, Spud, but I think we should find somewhere that's ready," said the man.

"Oh no! Don't go!" pleaded Spud. "It's lunchtime! This way to the hotel restaurant. You won't be sorry."

The family were hungry, so they followed Spud down the stairs. He dashed into the empty kitchen.

After making an awful mess of the kitchen, Spud finally had three bowls of spaghetti ready. He put on a waiter's outfit and went into the restaurant to serve the guests. He didn't get very far. He slopped and slipped, landing on the floor, covered in spaghetti sauce.

Kindly, the family told Spud they would come back another day. Spud knew he had ruined the opening day of the hotel. He went to seek Bob's help.

Bob and Wendy had just finished putting the doors on the villas. They were looking great!

Spud ran up mumbling something about guests and things going wrong. Bob knew Spud had been up to something he shouldn't have been!

"If it were me, Spud," said Bob. "I'd offer those guests somewhere nice to stay ..."

"Like one of these villas," agreed Wendy.

Spud looked at the comfy villas and knew it was the perfect solution. He rushed off to find the family.

Meanwhile, Lewella and Packer had returned with the beds, and Dickie Chester, the new hotel manager, had arrived. Now all they needed was guests!

Luckily, the family had agreed to return with Spud. When they came back, Dickie Chester welcomed them to Bobland Bay.

"Will you be staying, too?" the little boy asked Spud. He found Spud really funny.

"No," replied Spud. "I have crows to scare." He'd had enough of hotels for one day!

Where Did I Put It?

Bob has lost some of his things. Can you see them in the picture? Circle them when you find them.

Answers on page 68.

Shadow Play

Can you help Wendy match the machine with its shadow?
Draw a line to match up each one.

Answers on page 68.

A Perfect Promenade

One sunny morning, Tumbler arrived to help the team.

"You're going to need loads of cement for the new Bobland Bay promenade," he told them.

Bob explained that a promenade was a wide pavement with gardens and fountains. It would run along the seashore and be a place for everyone to go to enjoy the sea.

"We could make it even better by adding a special design or something," suggested Wendy. They all agreed it needed a Bobland Bay touch, but what could it be?

As they drove to Bobland Bay, the ground was so bumpy that Muck accidentally dropped and broke some of the paving slabs. It wasn't his fault but he was very sorry.

"I'll go back to the yard and make some more," suggested Wendy to Bob. Tumbler went with her to help.

As Wendy and Tumbler were waiting for the cement to set, Bob called on the talkie-talkie.

"We're really busy, Wendy. Can you come back?" he asked.

"I can stay and look after the slabs, Wendy," offered Tumbler.

"Thanks, Tumbler," she said.

She left him on slab watch, trying to think up a special promenade idea.

While Tumbler was waiting for the paving slabs to set hard, three birds flew into the yard. Tumbler was delighted to have some company. He went towards them but scared the birds and they took flight. They landed a few metres away, in the cement!

"Oh no, Birdies!" cried Tumbler. "Wendy said I shouldn't let anyone walk on the slabs. How do I explain bird footmarks in the cement?" But then some rabbits came along and walked over the slabs too. Keeping guard wasn't going well for Tumbler!

Meanwhile, back at the seafront, the promenade was almost finished. Muck reminded Bob and Wendy that they needed to collect the new paving slabs from the yard.

"I'll go, Wendy," said Bob. "Why don't you work on the promenade idea while we're gone. We've still got time."

Lofty gave Bob a lift.

At the yard, Tumbler had been joined by Spud. He told Spud all about the birds and bunnies ruining the slabs and how he hadn't thought of a single idea yet.

"You need a brainy scarecrow's help!" cried Spud. He closed his eyes and tapped his head to wake up his brain. But with his eyes closed, Spud couldn't see where he was going...

When Bob and Lofty arrived, they saw Spud fall headfirst into a wet paving slab. As he got up, he grabbed his face.

"My nose," he cried. "It's gone!"

Spud's parsnip nose was still in the cement!

Tumbler started to sob. "I had an easy peasy job to do and I've messed it up!"

Bob looked at the animal footprints in the other slabs.

"But Tumbler," he said. "Wendy will love these prints!"

Tumbler looked at the slabs again. Suddenly he saw what Bob meant. "Why don't we all make prints!" he said.

So that's what they did! Muck left his big track. Scoop left a tyre print and Dizzy put in her two front wheels. Wendy *was* delighted.

"Tumbler, these slabs are fantastic!" she said, helping Bob to put them into place on the promenade.

There were two slabs left. One for Bob and one for Wendy.
They bent down and made handprints in the wet cement.

"It's the Bobland Bay Walk of Fame!" said Tumbler.

"It's that special Bobland Bay touch!" exclaimed Wendy.
"How did you come up with such an amazing idea?"

"I don't know," admitted Tumbler. "It just sort of happened." And as he said it, the bunnies and birds appeared. They bounced around Tumbler, happy to be part of the Bobland Bay Walk of Fame.

Answers

Page 12 Guess Who

a) Wendy

b) Farmer Pickles

c) Spud

a) Mayor Bentley

c) Meg

a) Lewella

b) Dickie Chester

b) Paolo

Page 20 Who Lives Where?

Page 29 Spot the Difference

Page 36 Mucky Muck's Maze

Page 37 The Shapes Game

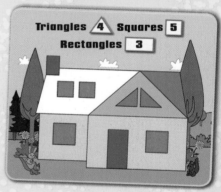

Triangles **4** Squares **5**
Rectangles **3**

Page 38 Colour Mix-up

Page 52 Whose Wheels?

Page 53 Join the Dots

Page 60 Where Did I Put It?

Page 61 Shadow Play